y Anna Kang *illustrated by* Christopher Weyant

This Is (Not) Enough

 • Published by Two Lions, New York • www.apub.com • Amazon, the Amazon logo, and Two Lions are trademarks of Amazon.com, Inc., or its affiliates. • ISBN-13: 9781542018517 • ISBN-10: 154201851X • The illustrations are rendered in ink and watercolor with brush pens on Arches paper. • Book design by Abby Dening • Printed in China • First Edition • 10 9 8 7 6 5 4 3 2 1

Yes!

To our brave and selfless
healthcare workers, first responders,
essential workers, scientists, and beloved
teachers. Thank you for your sacrifice,
the gift of everything.

This is
not enough.

Did you find
a present yet?

Not yet.

This is for my best friend!
It has to be COOL and FUN
and BIG and "WOW"!

Like *this*!

Wow!

What are you going to get?
I am not sure yet.

But it has to be
one of a kind.

And warm
and soft.

And from
the heart.

It has to be
something that
shows how
I *feel*!

I know! I am going to knit a one-of-a-kind, warm, soft, from-the-heart scarf!

Good idea!
Can you knit?
How hard
can it be?

I can't WAIT for you
to see your gift!

Well, I have the BEST idea for *your* gift!

What is it?
You will find out soon enough!

This is not enough.

And then you write,
"Thank you for being my best friend!"

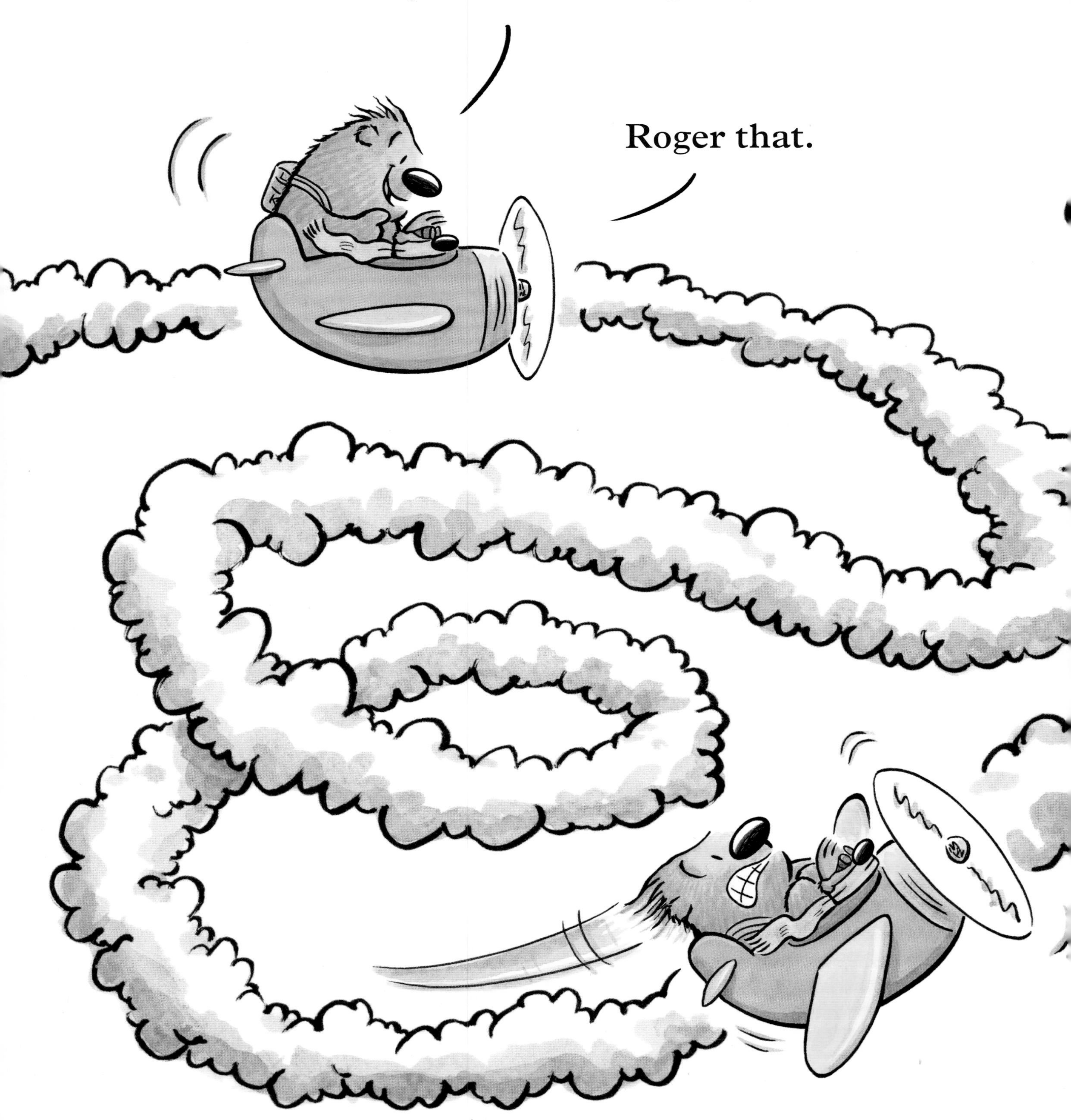

AHHHHHHH!
Never mind! EJECT!
I've *got* it!

What is all this?

You will find out
soon enough!

HOW
TO
KNIT

Sigh. This is not good enough.

LATER
INSTANT MAGICAL GARDEN
INSTANT MAGICAL GARDEN
INSTANT MAGICAL GARDEN

EASY
CAKE

BUMP!

THIS IS NOT

ENOUGH!!!

Close your eyes!

Okay, open them!

TA-DA!

You *made* this?
For *me*?
Yes!

It is so cool and fun
and big and "wow"!
I *LOVE* it!

I wanted to give you something one of a kind. And warm. And soft. And from the heart.

Something that showed you how I *feel*.

It is not enough, but all
I have is this. . . .

You *made* this?

Yes.

It is more than enough.

It is everything.

Surprise!
What did you get *us*?